YiKES!!!

Robert Florczak

THE BLUE SKY PRESS · An Imprint of Scholastic Inc. · New York

I'm going on a journey through wild and dangerous places!

YiPPEE!

After a journey through
wild and dangerous places...

...it's good to be back home.

The fascinating animals, insects, and spiders pictured in this book live in a broad range of habitats—all over the world! You would never be able to see them all in one day—unless, of course, you visited a zoo or wildlife animal preserve. Most people rarely encounter these creatures in the wild, but you can have great fun learning more about them from books, magazines, and videos. Here are a few interesting facts.

RAINBOW LORIKEET. Parrot. Lives in Australia and nearby islands. Eats flowers, seeds, nectar, and insects.
 Also pictured: ring-tailed lemur* (primate; Madagascar), Philippine tarsier* (primate; Philippines), common chameleon (lizard; found from Europe to Africa to Asia), and emperor dragonfly (insect; found from Europe to Africa, the Middle East, and Asia).

KOMODO DRAGON.* Giant monitor lizard. Lives in Indonesia. Eats a range of animals including deer, birds, fish, pigs, and water buffalo. Can weigh nearly 550 pounds.
 Also pictured: praying mantis (insect; found widely from Africa to Europe, Asia, and North America).

THAI COBRA. Venomous snake. Lives in the rainforests of Thailand. Also found in villages and cities where it kills hundreds of humans each year. Eats lizards, rodents, and small animals.
 Also pictured: walking stick (insect; found in tropical regions worldwide).

ORANGUTAN.* Primate. Lives in the forests of Borneo and Sumatra. Eats vegetation, fruit, and bird eggs. Can weigh more than 200 pounds.
 Also pictured: Hercules beetle (insect; equatorial rainforests).

BATS. Winged mammals. Live primarily in tropical regions but can be found worldwide. Most species feed on insects or fruit; however, vampire bats feed on the blood of cows, pigs, and other live animals.
 Also pictured: cave centipede (insect; found in warm regions worldwide).

BENGAL TIGER.* Big cat. Lives in India and Southeast Asia. Eats a range of animals, including birds, pigs, deer, and water buffalo. Can grow to 10 feet long.
 Also pictured: yellow jungle nymph (insect; Malay Peninsula).

EMERALD TREE BOA. Nonvenomous snake. Lives in South America. Eats rodents and birds. Can grow to more than 7 feet.
 Also pictured: leaf-footed bug (insect; Southern Brazil).

EMPEROR SCORPION. Venomous arachnid. Lives in coastal West Africa. Stings and eats other insects and small animals. Can grow to 6.5 inches in length.
 Also pictured: giant tiger centipede (insect; Africa).

NILE CROCODILE.* Reptile. Lives in southern Africa and Madagascar. Eats primarily fish as well as animals as large as hippos and wildebeests. Can grow as long as 20 feet and weigh nearly 500 pounds.
 Also pictured: African tick (insect; Africa).

MOUNTAIN GORILLA.* Primate. Lives only in the highlands bordering Congo, Rwanda, and Uganda. Eats vegetation, fruit, and insects. Can weigh more than 500 pounds.
 Also pictured: hunting wasp (insect; Africa).

RED-LEGGED TARANTULA. Venomous spider. Lives in Mexico. Uses its fangs to kill and eat small animals. Can grow to 7 inches across.
 Also pictured: biting horse fly (insect; found in swampy regions worldwide).

MONKEY-EATING EAGLE.* Raptor. Lives in the Philippines. Eats monkeys and other small animals. Can weigh up to 14 pounds.
 Also pictured: king cobra (world's largest venomous snake; found in tropical rainforests and grasslands of India and Southeast Asia).

BIRD-EATING GIANT ORB WEAVER. Venomous spider. Lives in Madagascar. Eats small birds and bats that it catches in its large web.
 Also pictured: tiger moth caterpillar (insect; found worldwide).

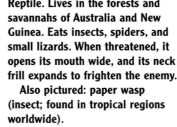

AUSTRALIAN FRILLED LIZARD. Reptile. Lives in the forests and savannahs of Australia and New Guinea. Eats insects, spiders, and small lizards. When threatened, it opens its mouth wide, and its neck frill expands to frighten the enemy.
 Also pictured: paper wasp (insect; found in tropical regions worldwide).

A boy with his dog.
 Also pictured: squirrel (rodent; found worldwide), northern oriole (songbird; U.S. and southern Canada), monarch butterfly (insect; North and South America, Australia and nearby islands).

*Endangered or threatened species according to the U.S. Fish & Wildlife Service.

FOR CHARLOTTE ROHREN

The Blue Sky Press   Copyright © 2003 by Robert Florczak   All rights reserved.   No part of this publication may be reproduced, or stored in a retrieval system, or transmitted in any form or by any means, electronic, mechanical, photocopying, recording, or otherwise, without written permission of the publisher.   For information regarding permission, please write to: Permissions Department, Scholastic Inc., 557 Broadway, New York, New York 10012.   SCHOLASTIC, THE BLUE SKY PRESS, and associated logos are trademarks and/or registered trademarks of Scholastic Inc.   Library of Congress catalog card number: 2002006551   ISBN 0-590-05043-5   10 9 8 7 6 5 4 3 2 1   03 04 05 06 07   Printed in Singapore   46   First printing, September 2003   Special thanks to Dr. Nancy B. Simmons at the American Museum of Natural History.   The illustrations were created in TOMBOW™ markers, colored pencils, and gouache on brownline paper.   Hand-lettering by David Coulson   Designed by Kathleen Westray